This year for Christmas you might find,
a lot on Santa Claus's mind

Like how to deliver presents, while keeping safe social distance.

His reindeer sleigh or snow sled...
his cloth mask wrapped around his head.

Singing out loud...ho ho ho.
It's Social Distance Santa yo!

This year might mean less family....
but we can love what we can't see.

You can still write Christmas cards.
They're safe to send both near and far.

Deliver with care, social distance Santa,
cards to loved ones…. Hi Nana!

When Santa fills stockings with care, will hand sanitizer be in there?

Santa loves milk and cookies.
With chocolate chips? Um, Yes please!

If you shop for a Christmas tree, please practice social distancing.

Is it Santa or someone's job,
to get that Christmas drink Eggnog?

To social distance... old Saint Nick

might recommend outdoor picnics.

We'll see Santa every year,
and celebrate with Christmas cheer.

Time out on all electronics,
when opening our Christmas gifts.

This year instead... or with a toy.
I wish for Christmas to spread joy.

That Santa and cute Christmas elves,
save some presents for themselves.

And remember...
Santa says that on Christmas,
Love conquers any distance!

Author Books

Be sure to check out other fun and spirited children's books
by author Eric DeSio available at www.BeYouBooks.com

Made in the USA
Monee, IL
23 November 2020

49121495R00017